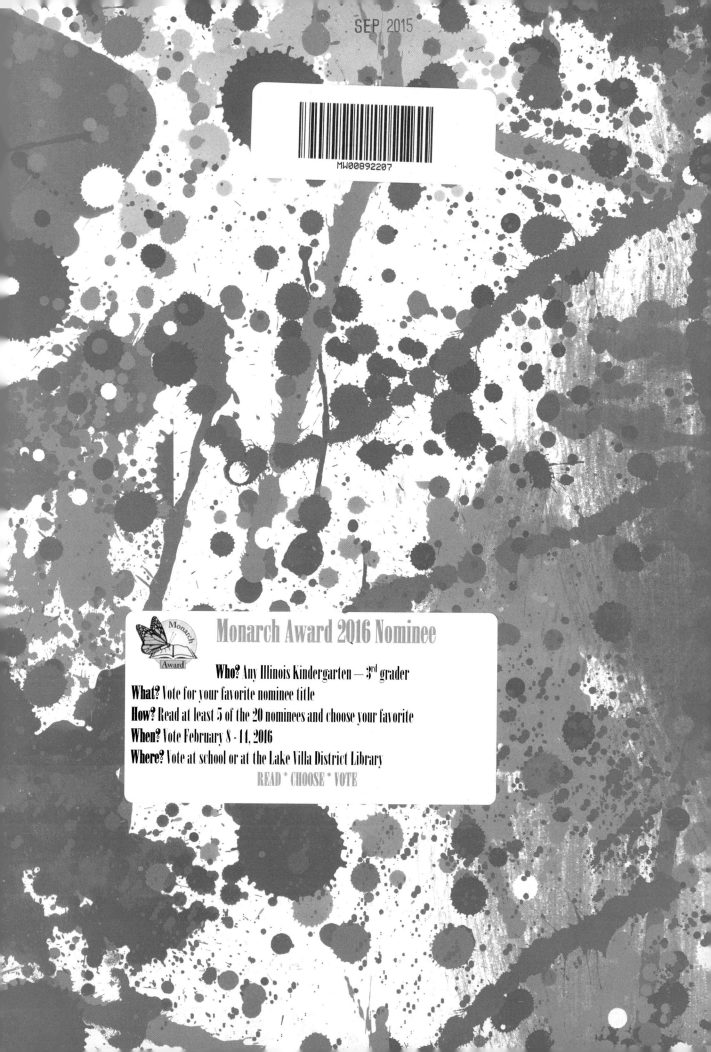

Monarch Award 2016 Nominee

Who? Any Illinois Kindergarten — 3rd grader

What? Vote for your favorite nominee title

How? Read at least 5 of the 20 nominees and choose your favorite

When? Vote February 8 - 11, 2016

Where? Vote at school or at the Lake Villa District Library

READ * CHOOSE * VOTE

THE GIRL WHO HEARD COLORS

Marie Harris • illustrated by Vanessa Brantley-Newton

Nancy Paulsen Books
An Imprint of Penguin Group (USA) Inc.

Jillian loved the world
with **all** her five senses.

She loved the tickling **touch**
of her bunny's whiskers on
her cheek.

an do this too

She loved the **taste**
of warm maple syrup
on waffles.

She loved the **smell**
of wet grass.

She loved the **sight**
of wild geese flying
across the blue sky.

And she loved the **sound**
of their honking.

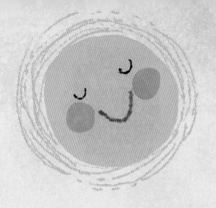

But what she loved most of all was seeing
the colors of everything she heard.

When she heard a dog barking,
she saw **bright red**.

When she rang the bell
on her bike, she saw silver.

The wind in the pine trees
blew soft gray.

The rain sang light purple.

Soon Jillian was old enough to go to school.

She loved school with **all** her five senses.

She loved the cool, slippery **feel**
of the floor and the tart **taste**
of her apple at snack time.

She loved the **smell**
of markers when her teacher
wrote on the whiteboard.

And still she saw the colors
of everything she heard.

The sound of the school bell
was as orange as a pumpkin.

RING!

RECESS!

Her teacher's voice
was as green
as a frog.

At recess, the children sounded as **gold** and **brown** as the leaves on the trees.

Then one day, something strange happened.
A lunch box dropped on the floor and
everything in it fell out with a loud clatter.

"What was that?" asked the teacher.

YELLOW!

Jillian replied.

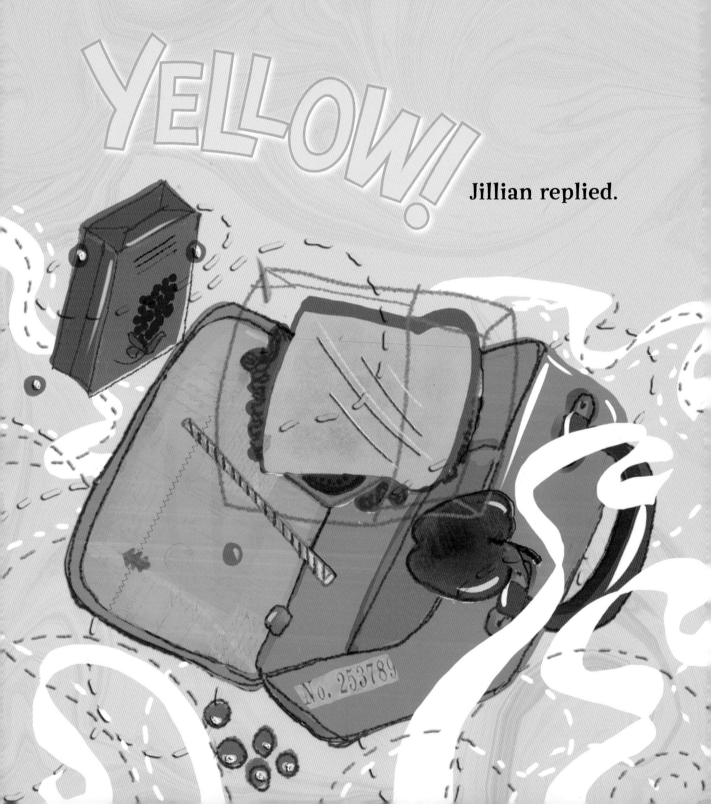

The children stopped what they were doing and looked at her.

"Yellow? A spilled lunch box is yellow?"

They began to laugh at Jillian.

Jillian felt sad with **all** her five senses.

She **felt** the warm tears on her cheeks.

She **tasted** the salt of her tears
on her tongue.

She **smelled** the spilled grape juice.

The children laughed harder and harder.

When she heard their laughter,
she saw **inky black**.

Her teacher was worried,
so she told Jillian's parents.

Jillian's parents were worried,
so they took her to the doctor.

The doctor examined her
eyes and ears.

There was nothing
wrong with them.

"Whatever could be wrong with Jillian?" everyone wondered.

Jillian whispered softly to herself: "I am as sad as a cloud."

Then came Music Day. The musician
opened his bag of instruments.
He handed out tambourines and
cymbals. Tin whistles and cowbells and
maracas and drums. The children took
turns playing all the instruments.

Except Jillian. She covered her ears and
squeezed her eyes shut.

"What's the matter?" asked the children.

"What's the matter?" asked her teacher.

"What's the matter?" asked the musician.

And Jillian said,

"I am hearing too many colors at once."

"Hearing colors?" the children exclaimed.
"What do you mean?"

"When I hear sounds, I see colors,"
Jillian told them.

"Me too!" said the musician
excitedly. "When I hear
sounds, I see colors too!
In fact, lots of people have a
very special extra sense.
It even has a name of its own:
synesthesia."

When Jillian heard the musician say
that word, she saw every shade of blue.
She began to smile.

Then the musician smiled.
Her teacher smiled. And all
the children smiled.

Jillian loved the world again
with **all** her five senses.

And her special extra one.

A few years ago, as part of my author visits, I began asking students a simple question: *What color is seven?* Most of the girls and boys looked at me in confusion, but every so often someone would answer *red* or *green* or *light brown*. Sure enough, she would be able to tell me the color of any number I named. Sometimes there would even be another student in that class who had colored numbers, but his would be completely different.

This "special extra sense" is called **synesthesia**, and if you have it, you might:

- hear the colors of music, voices and other sounds
- see the colors of numbers and letters, days of the week and months of the year
- taste sounds or shapes
- smell colors
- feel textures in color

Here are some ways my students explain their special sense:

- *My synesthesia is mostly with numbers. When I hear a number, it automatically flashes in my mind as a certain color.*
- *I know that letters in a book are black, but I see them in color when I read.*
- *My teacher's voice is waves of green with sparkles.*
- *It isn't distracting. In fact, having synesthesia helps me remember what I read.*
- *I felt afraid to tell anyone in case I would be teased, but now I realize that I'm not alone. Now I feel special and proud of my extra sense.*

This story is dedicated to the real-life Jillian, the very first synesthete I ever met; and in recognition of Amy Beach, America's first female composer, who heard colors and transformed them into extraordinary music. —M.H.

Thank you, Ha-Shem, for our five senses. For my children, Ben, Zoe and Chyna, with all my love. —V.B.-N.

NANCY PAULSEN BOOKS An imprint of Penguin Young Readers Group.
Published by The Penguin Group. Penguin Group (USA) Inc., 375 Hudson Street, New York, NY 10014, USA.

Text copyright © 2013 by Marie Harris. Illustrations copyright © 2013 by Vanessa Brantley-Newton.
Published simultaneously in Canada. Manufactured in China by South China Printing Co. Ltd.

Design by Ryan Thomann. Text set in Homemade Text. The artwork was digitally illustrated with Corel Painter 11 and Photoshop C5.

Library of Congress Cataloging-in-Publication Data
Harris, Marie. The girl who heard colors / Marie Harris ; illustrated by Vanessa Brantley Newton.
pages cm Summary: "Because she has a special extra sense called synesthesia, Jillian sees colors whenever she hears sounds"
—Provided by publisher. [1. Synesthesia—Fiction. 2. Senses and sensation—Fiction.] I. Newton, Vanessa, illustrator. II. Title.
PZ7.H24226Gi 2013 [E]—dc23 2012048221
ISBN 978-0-399-25643-1   10 9 8 7 6 5 4 3 2 1

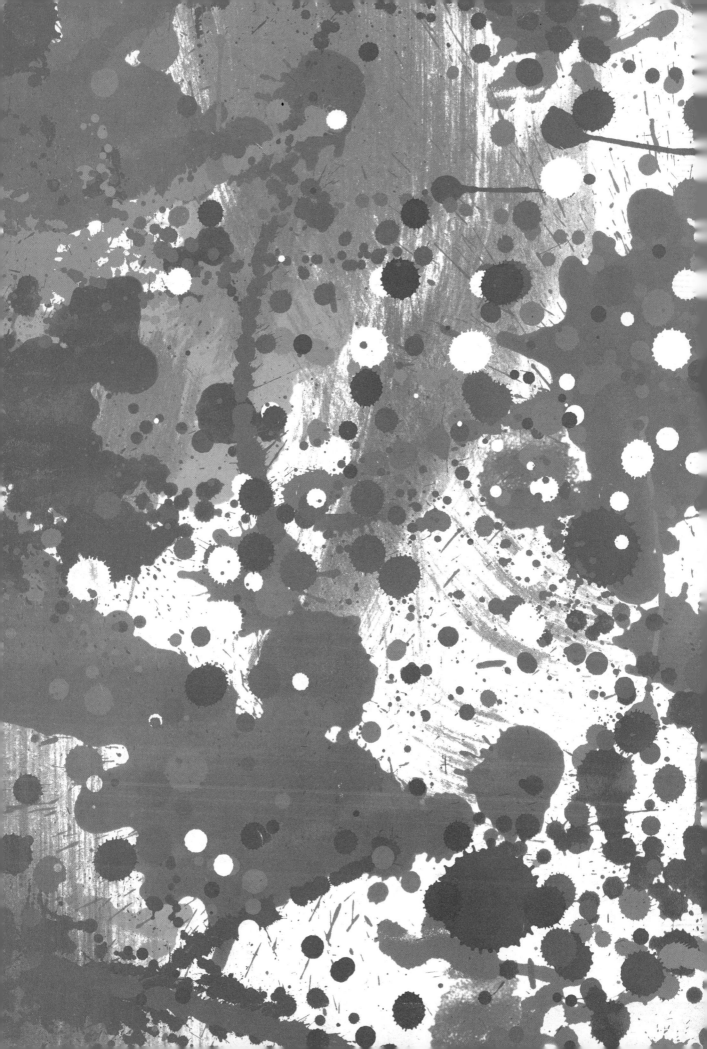